Scottish Terrier

Cross-breed

Ibizan Hound

Saluki   Chihuahua   Pug   Poodle

Bull Terrier   Chinese Crested   Bulldog   Dalmatian

For El

First published in 2009
by Macmillan Children's Books
a division of Macmillan Publishers Limited
20 New Wharf Road, London N1 9RR,
Basingstoke and Oxford
Associated companies
throughout the world
www.panmacmillan.com
ISBN 978-1-5098-0151-0
Text and illustrations copyright
© Emily Gravett 2009
The right of Emily Gravett
to be identified as the
author and illustrator of
this work has been asserted
by her in accordance
with the Copyright, Designs
and Patents Act 1988.

Printed in China
1 3 5 7 9 8 6 4 2

DOGS

Emily Gravett

MACMILLAN CHILDREN'S BOOKS

I love dogs.

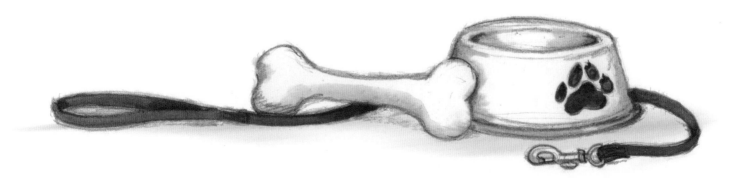

I love big dogs

and small dogs.

I love stroppy dogs

and soppy dogs.

I love dogs that bark

and dogs that don't.

I love dogs that play

and dogs that won't.

I love hairy dogs

and bald dogs.

Stripy dogs

and spotty dogs.

I love slow dogs

and fast dogs.

Scruffy

and smart dogs.

I love dogs that are good

and dogs that are bad.

But the dog that I love best?
Let's see . . .

. . . is any dog

that won't chase me!

Great Dane   Dachshund   Shar Pei